Elizabeth

– so lovely to have our energies commune! ♡

you fly so high but live on the ground –

Beautiful.

Love + light – enjoy the "journey".

[signature]

AuthorHouse™
1663 Liberty Drive
Bloomington, IN 47403
www.authorhouse.com
Phone: 1-800-839-8640

This book is based on the work of Paul and Gail Dennison.
The Brain Gym® movements are from Brain Gym®: Teacher's Edition, Revised, © 1989, 1994, and 2010 by Paul and Gail Dennison, and Brain Gym®: Simple Activities for Whole-Brain Learning, © 1986 by Dennison and Dennison. The activities, as well as the variations and descriptions suggested here, are used with permission.

Brain Gym® is a registered trademark of the Educational Kinesiology Foundation/Brain Gym® International, http://www.braingym.org. For permissions regarding the Brain Gym® books, contact:

Permissions Department
Edu-Kinesthetics, Inc.
P.O. Box 3396
Ventura, CA 93006-3396
www.braingym.com

The activities and techniques described in these pages are solely for educational purposes and are not intended as a diagnosis or prescription for any therapeutic purpose. They are meant to be easy, fun and comfortable to perform, and to complement, support and enhance your experience of whole brain learning. It is recommended that you consult your medical professional before beginning any exercise program.

First published by AuthorHouse 12/14/2011

ISBN: 978-1-4634-2332-2

Library of Congress Control Number: 2011916514
Printed in the United States of America

This book is printed on acid-free paper.

Into Great Forest

A Brain Gym® Journey

Written By Shelley Petch
Illustrated by Deanna Winter

WHAT IS BRAIN GYM?

The Brain Gym program is an innovative educational process. It is designed to help stabilize the individual's orienting system, ground one's physical structure, and provide effective tools for self-calming and self-management. The 26 movements are one of many important components within the program. These targeted activities recall the movements naturally done during the first years of life when learning to coordinate the eyes, ears, hands, and whole body. People continually report that they bring about rapid and often dramatic improvements in: concentration, memory, reading, writing, organizing, listening, physical co-ordination and more. Today the Brain Gym program, which has been recommended by educators for more than 20 years, continues to support people of all ages and abilities. It is used in more than 80 countries, and is taught in public and private schools world wide as well as in corporate, performing arts and athletic training programs. For more information, contact the non-profit organization: Brain Gym® International at www.braingym.org.

HOW TO USE THIS BOOK!

Enjoy this book as a story book initially. Because children relate so well to animals we felt it would be fun for the critters to teach these Brain Gym movements. By referencing the Appendix at the back of the book, the reader will learn the specifics of each movement and be able to properly use them while reading through the book. In time the child may simply flip to a random page and do the specific movement shown there or trace their way around the map, stop on some and do that particular movement. It is fun to allow the children to pick their own animals/movements. You will notice the movements are divided up into the three dimensions and color coded to match the pathways in the pictures. When your knowledge of the Brain Gym work increases you will be able to use the book in more in-depth ways. This could be a useful tool for any classroom teacher. It goes hand in hand with the Brain Gym®: Teacher's Edition which provides a much deeper explanation of the movements and their relationship to learning and behavior. For courses on Brain Gym or where to buy books, check the Brain Gym® website: www.braingym.org.

Let your imagination go and enjoy this Great Forest with all it has to offer!

Into Great Forest
A Brain Gym® Journey
Contents

Part One – The Golden Pathway: Midline Movements

Part Two – The Bronze Pathway: Energy Exercises and Deepening Attitudes

Part Three – The Copper Pathway: Lengthening Activities

Welcome to Great Forest! Come with us on a journey to meet the animals. They each have something to show us.

The Wise Man of the Great Forest is giving us our first map to guide us along the Golden Pathway.

Buffalo live in herds and are happy to share with one another.
The young one is doing The Cross Crawl.
She finds that this helps her to listen and see better,
and to have balance in her life.

How many foxes can you see? They are clever, quick and good at hiding. The mother fox needs to see very well to watch her busy family, so to sharpen her vision she likes to draw Lazy 8s in the sand.

These weasels are enjoying the sunrise. One of them is still and quiet while she looks around. The other one is doing The Rocker so he can focus well and have more energy to play.

The full moon is a beautiful thing to see. One wolf is talking by howling to his brothers far away. The other wolves are doing Neck Rolls to relax their muscles so they can see, hear, and think clearly for their hunt.

Look quickly and you will see this butterfly doing
The Double Doodle. As she does, she notices that her
flight is fast and light, and she knows just where she is
in space.

Shhh. . . Let's be very quiet while this orangutan does his Belly Breathing. He likes the way he feels calm and alert after he is finished.

What is this little opossum doing? She is using Cross Crawl Sit-ups. She finds this helps her when she wants to move quickly and smoothly.

We come now to a sunny rock where this lizard loves to dream. As he uses The Energizer, he finds that his thinking becomes clear and that he can understand things more easily.

Elephants have long trunks, large ivory tusks, and good memories.

The Elephant draws Lazy 8 shapes in the air to remember things well, and to relax her neck.

Would you like to sit and have some blueberry juice?

Once we have rested, the Wise Man will give us our second map to show us the way along the Bronze Pathway.

Here sit two pandas. When it is time for them to be calm and peaceful, they like to practice Hook-ups.

This joyful little porcupine loves her toys. Before playing, she does Brain Buttons to see well, relax, and balance herself.

Do you ever feel scared? Rabbits are often nervous or afraid. This rabbit is touching The Positive Points so he can let go of his fears.

Squirrels travel with awesome speed through the treetops and never fall. By holding her Balance Buttons, this squirrel makes sure that her balance is at its best.

If you peek inside that tree you will see a bat. By doing The Thinking Cap he finds that he can think clearly about what he hears, and pay attention to only the most important sounds.

Here we see the lynx. When his jaw feels tense, he enjoys doing The Energy Yawn. He notices that this helps him express himself well and chew his food more easily.

Look at the proud, strong camels. These creatures are also soft and gentle. They live in the hot, dry desert, and they know how important Sipping Water is to a healthy, well-functioning body and mind.

The eyes of the eagle are steady and help him to see far away. Eagles live their lives both high in the sky and down on the land. This eagle finds that Space Buttons sharpen his vision and help him to know where he is.

By holding Earth Buttons this grouse finds that she can move with more harmony and balance, and does not bump into anything when she dances.

Look how well her friend is doing a beautiful spiral dance.

We have come very far. The Wise Man is waiting to give us the last map, to show us the way along the Copper Pathway.

He has a special gift for you when we reach the end of this journey through Great Forest.

Mother moose is encouraging the young moose as he does The Gravity Glider. He wants to be confident, graceful, and have good balance like his parents.

Now our journey takes us into the northern night. The polar bear lives here. To catch his food, he needs to be calm and quiet. He finds that by doing The Grounder he feels stable, balanced, and focused.

Up on a ledge we see a mountain lion doing The Calf Pump. She enjoys the way that it helps her to pay better attention, to get along well with others, and to get ready to run when she needs to.

Doing The Footflex is this kangaroo's way to listen, learn, and express herself well. Then she can bound through her life without holding back.

Spiders are very good at creating. They make beautiful webs.
Here we see a spider using Arm Activation, since she finds
it improves her ability to make both big and little movements.
Then she can spin her very best.

Owls can see well at night. They can see what others cannot. By practicing The Owl, this wise bird notices his neck relax, and his focus, memory, and eye movements improve.

We come out of the woods and we are back where we started!
Our travels through Great Forest have taken us in a big circle.

The Wise Man is very proud of you for taking this journey and wants to give you a complete map of Great Forest. Now you may choose any animal or Brain Gym movement whenever you like. Have fun!

N
W
E
S

How To Do The Animals' Favourite Movements

The following descriptions of each of the movements illustrated by the animals will assist the reader to accurately execute the movement.

Please refer to the Brain Gym®: Teacher's Edition 2010 to obtain more information about these movements.

<u>Part One - The Golden Pathway: Midline Movements</u>

<u>The Cross Crawl</u> - page 2 (of this book) - Similar to walking in place, alternately move one arm and its opposite leg and then the other arm and its opposite leg. For example: touch the right hand to the left knee, then the left hand to the right knee.

<u>Lazy 8s</u> - page 3 - With the left arm fully extended in front with the hand at eye level, allow the hand to trace or draw the image of an 8 on its side, moving counterclockwise up, over and around. Then in a continuous movement move clockwise up, over and around and back to the beginning midpoint. As the eyes follow the Lazy 8, the head moves slightly and the neck remains relaxed. Repeat 3 times with each hand then with both together.

<u>The Rocker</u> - page 4 - May be done while sitting on a comfortable padded surface or on the edge of a chair to protect the tail bone. From a sitting position on a padded surface on the floor, lean back on forearms or hands for added support. With knees bent, rock in small circles first on one hip and then the other until the tension melts.

<u>Neck Rolls</u> - page 5 - Allow your head to slowly roll from side to side while breathing deeply. Imagine the chin is drawing a curved line on your chest from clavicle to clavicle but not pastthem. Release shoulders by rolling head with shoulders up, then again with shoulders down. Imagine the head is reaching out of the body rather than collapsing down. Do Neck Rolls with eyes closed, then open.

The Double Doodle - page 6 - This uses the large muscles of the arms and shoulders. Always refer to the physical midline for directional reference while saying "out, up, in and down" as you stand behind the child and guide their arms and hands to draw a square, circle or other shapes with both hands simultaneously. Set the child free when both hands are able to move together, mirroring each other easily, with relaxed head and eye movements. Encourage innovation & experimentation, beginning on a board in front of the child and progress to a piece of paper taped to the desk or floor. This could be done in front of you as conducting an orchestra.

Belly Breathing - page 7 - While standing straight, sitting, or lying flat, rest hands on the lower abdomen, inhale through nose (hands will rise on the belly), then exhale in short puffs through pursed lips (hands will fall in on belly). This one long slow breath will initially help to cleanse the lungs, the out breath will then always be done through the nose. Inhale to a count of three, hold for a count of three, exhale for a count of three. Repeat.

Cross Crawl Sit-ups - page 8 – Lying on the floor with knees bent (on a padded surface to protect your tailbone), cross your wrists to rest your arms on your chest. Reach with one elbow to the opposite, lifted knee, then continue alternating each elbow to its opposite knee as though riding a bicycle.

The Energizer - page 9 - Sit comfortably in a chair with your head forward resting on a table or desk. Place your hands on the desk in front of your shoulders fingers pointing slightly inward. As you inhale you experience your breath flowing up your midline like a fountain of energy lifting first your forehead, then neck and finally your upper back. The diaphragm and chest stay open and shoulders stay relaxed. Then to return, curl your head toward your chest and bring your forehead down to rest on the desk. Experience your breath as the source of your strength. Keep shoulders apart and relaxed. This can also be done lying face-down on a mat.

The Elephant - page 10 - "See" a lazy 8 in the distance in front of you. Relate the center and sides of the 8 to the shape in the environment i.e.: the center line of a chalkboard or a tree. Bend your knees and "glue" your head to one shoulder while you point your arm (elephant trunk) across the room. Use your ribs to move your whole upper body as you look past your fingers and trace the distant lazy 8 with your arm. No body twist is involved, and the hand may appear double or out of focus.

Part Two – The Bronze Pathway: Energy Exercises and Deepening Attitudes

Hook-ups - page 14 - Part One: Sitting, cross one ankle over the other. Extend the arms out in front of you with the backs of the hands touching. Cross one hand over the other so palms are touching and thumbs are pointing to the floor. Then interlace fingers and draw hands under and towards chest. Close eyes, breathe deeply and relax for about one minute. You may also press the tongue flat against the roof of your mouth on inhalation and relax tongue on exhalation.
Part Two: When ready, uncross the ankles and release hands simply touching fingertips of both hands together continuing to breathe deeply for another minute.

Brain Buttons - page 15 –Place one hand over your navel. Make a "U" shape with the other hand and place your thumb and index finger in the small depressions just below your collarbone and about one inch to each side of your breastbone. Rub the points at your collarbone for about 30 seconds as you move your eyes slowly to the left and right along a horizontal line. Continue with the other hand.

The Positive Points - page 16 - Lightly touch the points above the eyes half way between the eyebrow and the hairline (frontal eminences) with your fingertips. You may close your eyes and allow yourself to remember something like the spelling of a word or a potentially stress-producing situation. Once you have experienced the image or associated tension then experience its release. Someone else may hold yours. You may gently massage positive points to relieve visual stress. You may use these in conjunction with creative visualizations such as imagining a pleasant scene or creative thinking such as an alternative outcome to an event or story.

Balance Buttons - page 17 - Touch two fingers to the indentation at the base of the skull behind the ear and about 1 ½ to 2 inches from the spinal midline. Place the other hand over the navel. The chin is tucked in and the head is level. After a minute or so, switch to hold behind the other ear. You could also massage the back of the head.

The Thinking Cap - page 18 - With the thumb and index fingers gently pull the ears back to unroll them, beginning at the top of the ear and gently massaging them down and around the curve ending with the bottom lobe. Keep your head upright and chin comfortably level. Repeat this process three or more times.

The Energy Yawn - page 19 - Place your fingers over the cheeks where the back molars are. You will feel the large muscles just in front of the joints. Gently massage these muscles while pretending to yawn and deeply sigh aloud. Feel the muscles "melt" under your fingers. Repeat the activity 3-6 times.

Sipping Water - page 20 - You can feel your best by eating foods that contain natural water like fruits and vegetables and by drinking plenty of good clear water. All other liquids are processed in the body as foods and do not serve the body's water needs. A traditional way of figuring how much water one requires is to figure one ounce of water per day for every three pounds of body weight, doubling that in times of stress. It is best to discover for yourself what works best for your individual body. Ingest in small but frequent amounts. Water makes up roughly 70% of the human body and over 90% of the human brain so it is important to continually replace water and stay hydrated.

Space Buttons - page 21 - Both hands rest on the midline of the body – one hand is placed on the back midline (spine) just above the tailbone and the other hand on the front midline, fingertips above the upper lip. Breathe energy up your spine and experience the resulting relaxation. The points may be held for thirty seconds or more (4 - 6 complete breaths). Changing hands may help activate both sides of the brain. You may allow the eyes to track a vertical plane directly in front of you.

Earth Buttons - page 22 - Place at least two fingertips of one hand on the chin just under the lower lip, the other hand is placed on the navel with fingertips pointing down to the ground. They will rest about 6 inches below the navel at the top of the pubic bone. These points may be held for thirty seconds or more (4-6 complete breaths) while breathing slowly and deeply experiencing the relaxation. Change hands to activate both sides of the brain. You may look down (for grounding) while holding the buttons, then "walk" your vision up to a point in the distance or "walk" it up a vertical plane (floor to ceiling at a corner).

Part Three - The Copper Pathway: Lengthening Activities

The Gravity Glider - page 26 - Sit comfortably. Cross your ankles keeping your knees relaxed. Bend forward and reach out in front of you letting your arms glide down your legs exhaling. Float back up while inhaling. Repeat three times then cross ankles the other way and repeat three times. When you feel ready, do the Gravity Glider with your eyes closed or in a standing position keeping the knees unlocked and the low back flat.

The Grounder - page 27 - Position your feet about one leg length apart with feet at right angles to each other. Point your right foot to the right and point the left foot straight ahead. The bending right knee glides forward in a straight line out over (but not past) the forward facing right foot while exhaling. The torso and pelvis face straight ahead and only the lead knee and foot face sideways. This lengthens and strengthens the muscles along the inner hip and thigh of the straight leg and stabilizes the back. Repeat three times and then repeat on the left side.

The Calf Pump - page 28 - Stand supporting yourself with hands on a wall or back of a chair. Place one leg out behind you with foot flat on the floor while bending the knee of the front leg. Keep the back straight, inhale with weight on front leg and back leg is on the toe with heel off the floor. Next lower the heel to the floor shifting the weight to the back leg and exhale for at least a count of eight. Repeat three or more times on each side.

The Footflex - page 29 - Sitting with one ankle resting on the other knee, place your fingertips at the beginning and end of the calf muscle area. Visualize the tendons and muscles that run from behind the knee to the ankle are like clay and as you hold them apart and breathe out, they relax and "soften or melt". While you hold these points, breathe deeply and point and flex your foot slowly. Repeat with other foot and calf.

Arm Activation - page 30 - Hold one arm straight up in the air close to your ear. Grasp this extended arm with the other hand which is also up and bent so you can grasp the straight arm near the elbow. Exhale through pursed lips to a count of eight or more while activating the muscles in the straight arm by pushing against the hand of the bent arm in four directions (front, back, in and away). Take one or more complete breathes in each direction. This can be done sitting, standing or lying down. This can be done with arm up at 180 degrees or 90 degrees straight out in front or 45 degrees in front or straight down at your side. Notice any relaxation, vitality or coordination as arm tension is released.

The Owl - page 31 - Grasp the top of the shoulder and squeeze the muscles firmly. Turn your head to look back over your shoulder, breathing deeply and pulling your shoulders back. Next turn head smoothly across the midfield to the other shoulder keeping chin level. Exhale deeply each time the head is to each side and again when the head is in center and tilted forward releasing back-of the-neck muscles. Repeat with the other shoulder. Make a sound like the owl's "who-o-o-o" with each exhalation.

Our hope is for our readers, young and old, to reconnect with nature and allow these wondrous animals to teach us all. Through them we offer these Brain Gym® tools as a way to pursue integration back to our original, whole selves, so that we may live life to our full potential and allow lifelong learning to be easy and rewarding.

ACKNOWLEDGMENTS

∞ To my Dad, who always encouraged me. - Deanna Winter

∞ My husband Kip, who has been my greatest supporter and love.....no matter what!

∞ My children, Bryn and Karli, who have been my greatest teachers and the loves of my life. Thank you for leading me to find the Brain Gym® work and allowing me to practice on you until I grew to understand it's depth and profound genius.

∞ My parents who taught me compassion for all living things and encouraged me to question. Thanks Dad for your teachings of the interconnections of all that is.

∞ Gail and Paul Dennison for this important work and their belief and encouragement in this project. I am deeply grateful.

∞ Jamie Sams and David Carson for their insightful wisdom of the interconnectedness within the animal world, aptly illustrated in their Medicine Cards®.

∞ T. Harv Eker for his educational and life altering camps at Peak Potentials Training, that allowed me to break through to my core and recognize this book was even a possibility. Thank you for your living example of courage and miracles.

∞ The numerous Brain Gym® teachers and mentors along my journey. A huge thank you to Cindy Goldade and your review team for such patience and guidance in the project.

∞ All friends, colleagues, classmates and students who have supported me in many ways over the past several years of this creation.

∞ A huge thank you to Cara Alexander for her knowledge of the computer and design techniques. Your patience during the final editing is deeply appreciated.

∞ Lastly I wish to thank my artist friend Deanna, whose patience and love has inspired me and kept me on track when things weren't flowing. Your willingness to co-create is to be honored and admired. Thank you dear friend and long live the porcupine. -Shelley Petch